I Saw Her Foot

I saw her foot

Ludwig

ISBN 978-93-5458-876-1
© Ludwig 2021
Published in India 2021 by Pencil

Contributors:
Co-Author: Ludwig

A brand of
One Point Six Technologies Pvt. Ltd.
123, Building J2, Shram Seva Premises,
Wadala Truck Terminal, Wadala (E)
Mumbai 400037, Maharashtra, INDIA
E connect@thepencilapp.com
W www.thepencilapp.com

DISCLAIMER: *This is a work of fiction. Names, characters, places, events and incidents are the products of the author's imagination. The opinions expressed in this book do not seek to reflect the views of the Publisher.*

Author biography

About the author,

The book author 'Ludwig (AKA) 'Boobalan" is writes about world cinema essays. So far he has authored two books on cinema and one fiction novel. In addition, he has written some short stories. He is a part-time writer with a passion for writing. This is his first English language novel.

'Proud to show himself as an artist or writer, rather than to show his superiority in society in terms of economics and other qualifications.'

This is the beginning of a simple man who has nothing to do with writing and art. Through his passion and thirst for art, he has lost many things in himself. Still ready to lose. If there are any errors in writing or comment, we apologize.

CONTENTS

Acknowledgements

This is a story written based on philosophical thoughts. Humans' inner desires, preferences, needs, and rights are also manifested as dreams. The inner world of human beings does not always correspond to the outer world. This is a psychological fiction. The beginning of the 19th century was the heyday of philosophical thought.

Science and rationality were changing the world on the one hand, and philosophical ideas on the other were coming to Colossus in the West. Numerous fictions were written with the aim of embedding philosophical thought into logic.

Philosophical reasoning began to enter into science, not just stories. It can also be said that the very existence of logic is in question. Philosophical thought itself became the guide to the alignment of man's external world. It connected the inner world and the outer world in a straight line.

Based on that, the story, written in connection with the Lockdown period, unfolds into a fairytale world. The story is told by connecting the practical life external world and the dream life internal world in a straight line.

The first chapter of the novel summarizes the events closest to the whole non-fiction. The second chapter of the story alternates between fiction and reality. In the third chapter, fiction and reality run intertwined. The fourth chapter is entirely made up of fiction.

The story is told from the point of view of the protagonist. Simply through the dialogues, the scenes and events of the story unfold. It can even be said to be a theatrical running story.

Slightly exaggerated pornography may come up in the story. But, they are fictions related to the story, not unnecessary. This is an adult (18+) story. It's no surprise that this will definitely be a different treat for readers.

— Ludwig

I Saw Her Foot

CHAPTER - I

1.1 The Accommodation

— The decision to take the anger, the danger can only go.

 I do not need to advise you. You know everything for yourself.

— I already told him,

 'Be a little patient, everything will change. Time will never be the same '

He does not listen to anything.

— From now on he will listen. That is why I have come.

No problem.Stay here as long as you want.

No one will disturb you.

If anything bothers you, Call me right away.

— You won't have any problems, will you ?!

Because you have no problem keeping him here ?!

— Absolutely not!

As soon as Lockdown is over, I'll give him a good job at the same hotel where I work.

Let no one question you.

This is the place to stay for hotel workers.

If anyone asks a question, say you work at Hotel Euphoria.

(Even though both friends were comforting, I could not calm down.)

— No!

I don't feel like this is getting fixed.

I'm Leaving.

— Where are you going?

Don't act like a madman! Wherever you go at this time, the problem is yours.Be a little patient.

Tell me what you need?

Do you drink alcohol? Girl? Aunty ?!

— Hey .. don't talk ..

Just one job is enough. Trust me, refuse to give even a normal job? what a cruelty.

Have a job.

Need a small place to stay.

A small salary.

Enough is enough.

— No one will be working during this time.

Did you see I don't have a job?

If it was a normal day, do you know how many phone calls I would have received by this time ?!

I'm so free because it's Lockdown.

I'm still going. But not daily.

Because I am a technician, they only pay me for the days I go.

— He is saying that he will get a good job in the same hotel where he works ..

 What more could you want ..?!

 If you can get a job in a hotel, you can stay in this room permanently.

— Until then, are you telling me to close this room?

— You can be here freely.

Eat well. We often come and see you.

Be Mind relax. Don't think about anything! Do not confuse.

This is the room I was given to stay on behalf of the hotel as I work in a hotel.

I go home and come back daily.

— If Hotel Management knew, would you have any problems?

(I also accepted this question from a friend)

— No one knows.

Because I stayed in the same room daily. Go home only once a week ..

Let him trust you then.

— Can't I get a job somehow ?!

— What more can I say to comfort him ?!

Hmmm ... hey..don't go to that Room where the Opposite is ! It will be locked.

... Room with a guy who works at the bar.

He went to the town of Lockdown.

...This Hall, this Room, this Bathroom

You will not have Disturbance anywhere here.

— Okay shall I leave ?!

— Where are you going ?!

Stay with him for today.

Get some sleep and go home in the next morning.

I will come tomorrow too. Let's arrange for dinner.

We will drink alcohol tomorrow. Okay ?!

(He tries to clear my mind. I smiled approvingly at him too.)

— Who are these people?

— Are they? North Indians. Dishwashers at the hotel.

They were trapped in Lockdown. Staying here without being able to go home.

They have nothing to do with us. They are staying in the next apartment.

— Do we have this Full Apartment ?!

(The friend was overwhelmed with surprise.)

— Yes, an apartment house has two bed rooms, one hall, one kitchen, two balconies and one bathroom.

Allowed up to a maximum of 5 people. But there was only me and another boy in this hall.

This is Room with me, it is Room with him

..Mostly I will not stay here. I will go home. That guy alone will never move out of this Room.

— Buy me a job at that hotel and give it to me

He and I share this room.?!

— Why, what happened to the job you were looking at before?

— I'm home now!

— Do They Pay You From 'Work From Home'? Isn't it

— They only pay half the salary

— Well then all that can be done. First, let's make a way for him.

Be safe. I went home and made the call.

Is there a cigarette ?!

  (As we were talking, we lit a cigarette. 4 cigarettes are over.)

1.2 An Unexpected Night

— I need a bag.

— What is the bag that is already there?

— There is no zip in it, and it is torn.

— What do you have in that bag? Do you only have clothes ?!

— Yes, I need a good bag

— Where are you going now ?! Why do you need a good bag?

— I have no hope of getting a job here.

..I will only be here for a week. I am still staying here for the reason that he said consolation.

If I don't get any work in a week, I will definitely leave.

— Where ?!

— Book a Train Ticket and stay on the North side. Maybe Ladakh? Then I will go beyond that ..

— All right, go for a week, be patient here and see

— Who is here for me? !

To care about me and take care of my well-being ..

..Is there no one for me here?

— Without it, am I yours now ?!

If not, would he have given Room to stay?

hey, why are you looking at everything wrong ?!

You are thinking negatively .. you are making a sudden decision .. all this is done against you.

— Didn't I know I was like that?

Then why doesn't anyone understand me?

I mean be my dad, be my sister, why even be family with you

Did I have a bad name for everyone ?!

— You often fight with me. You disagree.

As a friend, I can follow you..

..But, will they do it? I do not know that.

— Just because I have no money, do they think I am trivial ?!

One day money will come to me too

— Yes, do it. Make way for survival.

After that, don't say I'm leaving and going nomadic!

— Well, I need a bag.

..I'm not going anywhere. I'm sorry to see this old bag.

— Do you have two bags for one ?!

For the nomadic person, if there are only two bags full of clothes, please take care ..

— No. I just want a Traveling Bag like this.

— Online ?!

— Is there cash on delivery ?! There will be no shop anywhere at this time!

Do you have any old bags ?!

— No!

— Maybe if you were online, would you order me and buy it for me ?!

Right away, awesome in three days.

— Well, come and see the balcony! What a scene!

(That night on the next floor, a young woman was drying clothes.)

— Did you call for this ?!

— All this to us, he did not say anything ?!

If you knew there was a beautiful woman next to the apartment, come here and stay!

Auntie has come, let's go.

(I noticed a faint sound in the room opposite. I went to the door and listened. Yes, there was a faint sound. Probably the sound of a fan inside the room.)

— Did you say that the room is locked ?!

— No. It is open .. Fan is running inside.

(After pushing a little, the door opened)

— hey .. you broke the door!

— I did not break. I think it is not locked properly.

— Look .. what's in the room ..

Holds bottles of wine as an exhibition.

— Didn't you remember that guy said he works at Hotel Bar?

— If you got a job at the same bar, Deily would do the same, wouldn't you?

(Throughout the room, it looked like it was stuffed. Even though the room looked clean and tidy, it was hard to even breathe. I opened the window. Even the window was covered with cloth.)

— What is all this ?! Has a lot of pictures stuck on the wall ?!

It is written as Zibu Symbol.

— I do not know. But is fine.

—If you wake up in the morning and look at these pictures from the bed as it is, how much peace of mind will be ?!

— All these pictures would have been even better if they had been in the hall.

— What's in that green bottle?

— Where ?!

— Signature ?!

— Is this wine? Water ?!

— hey Whiskey dude. Smell well.

— It seems so. But, be like perfume.

— Take a drop and put it on your tongue.

This is really good

Still don't know what's here. This Room is better than that Room. I would have liked.

Side dish also has almond, pista.

(We had a somewhat unexpected dinner that night)

1.3 Intimacy is interesting

— If someone asks you, tell them you came to buy a cake.

 When you come in, don't talk to anyone.

Let me come to the reception ..

— Excuse Me ..

— We have come to buy cake Sir.

— Go inside and make the right cut.

— Thanks Sir.

 (We entered)

— This is The Grand Hotel Euphoria

Have a Marriage Reception for today.

— Is this where you work?

— Not here, but on the Ground Floor.

— hey Swimming Pool. Did you see

— This is a 5 star hotel.

— Do you drink strawberry juice?

— This is not Strawberry. This is Raspberry

(I could not hear my friends talking. All my memories were floating elsewhere.)

— This is the seat for me. This is where everything is. Everything from here, can be tracked.

— Do you work for Camera Control Room?

— Is that what I said yesterday ?! Technician.

— Then tell me .. a lot of interesting things would have happened ?!

Have seen everything from here ..!

— No Camera Allowed in the room. But, there is a camera everywhere outside.

— What Range is available in this Hotel Room?

— Starting from 3000

  3000 to 1 lakh rupees.

— Is that all allowed here?

— For what?

— Is that Sex Work ?!

— It all happens normally here

— Wouldn't it be a problem if all this was known outside?

— Nothing will happen. Anyone, anyone can come together. Even if there is only proof. Whatever the problem, we know very well how to solve it.

An incident happened 3 weeks ago.

A politician, a good old man.50 years old. I do not know which party.

A little girl. Be 25 years old. Such a color.

Come straight. Take Room. To go inside.

Half an hour later, two women arrived at the reception.

... We should not give guest details to anyone else, that is the Rules.

But a madman told the truth at the reception.

— Who are those women?

— It's the wife and daughter of that politician.

— Then what ?!

— What the fuck ?!

The big problem exploded.

When they came out of the Room, everyone was on camera.

— Then what ?!

— She fell at the feet of the security. The women beat her and settled her mania

If we find out that something is wrong, we will record the relevant video.

— Is there such a big memory system here?

— All video will be with us for up to two weeks. Above that it will automatically become Erase..

Until then the relevant videos will be safe with us.

—Is that the video now ?!

—It's been 3 weeks.

Why is he speechless?

 (Their gaze fell on me)

— Can I get a job?

— That's why I came to you. You need to take a resume, tell me the details, I will type ..

— What did Details say?

— Where have you worked before? Your Address? Details for your Study?

— Where did I study. Even a degree like yours is hairdressing

— I recommend you myself

 hmm .. When doing the interview attent, wear a formal shirt.

— Let's see if the first job is available.

— hey, I know everyone in the HR Department. I have been working here for 5 years.

This Resume is for Formality only...

...This is because a lot of people will apply for the job once the lockdown is over...

... If you resume in advance, you will get the job first in the name of my recommendation. You need a job.

— Has anything else happened? Like this?

Has there been any Murder in this Hotel?

(When I heard that, friends froze for a moment.)

— I have heard that only one person I know has committed suicide.

That's all the resume is ready for me to finish work and go home.

1.4 The companion of loneliness

— How many more days until the 22nd?

— What about the 22nd ?!

 Six more days.

— It's the day Lockdown ends. Maybe, if the job is not available I will leave the next day.

— Are you counting the days?

— I will be patient. But, that beast I have inside will not have patience.

— Is that so ?!

— It will wake up on a full moon day. It does not sleep for more than a week before the full moon begins.

— Is that crazy ?!

 I can't stay here today.

May I come and see you tomorrow morning?

— Why ?!

— They keep calling from home.

— Tell me you're with me.

— No.

— Why is being with me, your family doesn't like it? - No, you shouldn't have fought that day.

— Did I fight you ?!

— It should not have been done in front of them.

— Oh .. you have family. I forgot. They remembered you just like me.

 You go .. don't come back ..

— Hey .. come tomorrow morning and see you.

— You lied and came here ?!

 Did I do something wrong?

You call me wrong today, you celebrated me before.

You said that there is no good man in the world like me..

..But now, you swear that there is no one in this world who is a bigger idiot than me

— Nobody does that.

— What's going on now ?! You and me. No matter how many places we went and stayed.

There is so much for you and me.

But, today you are listening to what your family has to say.

If you have me too you go spoiled, go

— Have you ever seen someone make a sudden decision and immediately express their anger? This is why no one likes you

— I'm been like this from the beginning.

— Nobody thinks you're wrong. You learn the life lesson first.

See you again in the morning.

(I sent him on his way and walked through the narrow city alleys)

— Everyone is a situationalist.

I can't lie. This is my nature.

(On the narrow road of the city, a feeling like I was stuck in the middle of the heights of buildings. I forgot the way.)

— This way?

That way ?? Forgot that Enclave name too ?!

Have a cigarette please..

— Which cigarette? There is only one brand

— Please give it to me..

— How many ?! No retail..

(I'm worried about the path)

— I have to choose a path

Wrong? Or Right ?

(The road I chose was the right one. It took me to where I was staying..

.. I felt lonely. I languished in the company of loneliness that night. This loneliness is not new to me. It's just coming and going from time to time.)

1.5 Fainting from alcohol

— What are you doing ?!

— I'm asleep

— Just come down

— I haven't bathed yet.

— Not going anywhere outside. Just Come on

(I went downstairs from the 4th floor to my friend)

— Look here, 15 bottles of wine. Everything is VSOP. The price is a bit high.

 I went to the nearest district and bought it.

A bottle, even if it sells for 350 rupees, is good.

Alcohol is rare at this time. What we say will be the price for this.

— Where to sell this to whom ?!

— Buy only 6 Bottle at Hotel.

The rest has to be sold to someone somehow.

— Well, what do I do now?

— I hide aside.

Someone will call you. Give him these 6 Bottle.

I already got paid. Do not get caught by the police. Go carefully.

— All right.

(We rode our bikes down the narrow streets)

— Who is this aunt?

— Where ?!

She is that shop aunt.

I just bought cigarettes here yesterday.

— Can you stand here?

(Last night, she could not see properly, Wearing glasses. Today she was head over heels in the afternoon light. When she turned around, I saw her feet. It was like a flower.)

— That aunt has no cracks in her feet!

— What is the problem if it is.?

— I do not like people with cracks in the feet.

That too good foot care at this age .. is a rare thing.

— Ha .. Ha ..

(I gave bottles of wine to someone who came in a two-wheeler from somewhere)

— Keep the spread 100 rupees for yourself

You have taken so much risk.

(Aunt came out of the shop and was sitting on the side of the road with her head down. She stumbled as she passed.)

— Bro, VSOP.. does anyone want it?

— How much do you pay?

— 350 ?!

— Nobody wants to buy that much here brother ..

That's 250.

— No Bro..

(We interrogated several people)

— All this is unnecessary work for me.

I borrowed from someone. There is no money to pay it back.

Something is my situation.

— only one bottle remained

— Take this and put it in the Room.

Tomorrow I will come to finish my work !

1.6 The Unselfish Act

- Do not hesitate.

Don't be afraid..speak something wrong or right ..

Tell me yourself

— Hmm ... I worked in Garments Company for 8 years.

— Speak out loud !

— I worked in Garments Company for 8 years.

  In this town, there are my friends. they said,

  'Stay with us here instead of going out and suffering!

— Did you get a good salary there ?!

Why are you trying here?

— Hmm .. just get paid a lot.

But, to close the company.

I have no one there.

— What are your parents doing ..?

— Mom died .. Dad Larry Driver.

 I have no understanding with him.

— Are you single now ..?

— Yup!

— You have a house, how do you get to work ..?

— I am staying at Friend's house. I will come as it is.

— How long can you come to this company from your home?

— Half-hour may come Sir.

— Well, give your resume.

You will not get the expected salary here.

 Hey, you're Fresher. You know nothing about this field.

 You take training. Training takes at least 3 months..

..Only then will you understand about this work..

..and you do not have a Degree Holder. So, there is no job that you thought of.

— All right sir.

— I just told you. Your salary is 7 thousand + BF

..Tell me if this condition is Comfortable.. You can join the work from Monday.

— I'm thinking Sir

— Hmm .. Do it anyway.

(I came out after the interview)

— Hey, what can I say?

— Did I ask you about this job?

Did you promise to buy a job at the hotel ?!

— Yes, but for a week you refuse to tolerate!

Why and what happened?

— I need a good salary. Accommodation, meals.

— okay leave it. This is also an attempt.!

Be patient. I will try in the hotel.

(A girl passed us)

— Come here sister ..

How far are you going?

— Going up to Junction.

— Here 50 rupees

..Buy something for the baby.

(She's gone)

— Who is she? Do you know her ?

— No. The child ran to the store to be by his side.

..But the girl did not leave the child

— Really ?!

— She would have been abandoned by her husband

Otherwise, she would have split up.

— How do you say.?

— They will even catch the cab and go.

But, In this way, two children should not be trapped and walked away ..

— But, is she all right?

  How did you predict this ?!

You have to be a detective.

You called her and without even knowing the situation with her, how did you immediately predict that she needed help ?!

It's amazing ..

— Everything is a prediction.

— Are you doing Absorb this thing ..?!

..They asked me inside too

— What?

— You've been out there all this time, have you noticed anything? That ..

— What did you say ?!

— I replied that I did not notice anything !

— Did you notice anything ?!

— Can I get a job?   I was thinking.

 But how, did you guess about her ?!

 - hey .. let it not a matter

 (I was surprised to think about my friend)

1.7 Everything Is an Illusion

— If I told you a secret, would you go and tell it to those involved ?!

I told you one thing as Personal.

Did you just go and tell her that ?!

— I didn't say anything.

— How did she know that thing?

— You would have told yourself!

— Don't act! how can I tell myself the wrong thing about her.?

I mean, a personal thing.

your my friend ? Not to her?

— I should not have gotten into the middle of a brother-sister fight. Why do you blame me?

— Who made you guilty?

I asked for money, that's true. But, I just asked for a credit.

She did not respect me as a Human Being.

You know her very well. You Supported for her

— I should not have interfered in this.

— What has this got to do with you and this problem ..?

Being a mediator, you only have to provide a neutral solution

If not, there must have been two people listening and talking.

Do not play Double Game.

— That's it, she says

There is justice on both sides.

— But, the only fault is mine..Is that so ?!

— She's in a lot of trouble herself.

Why bother her.?

— She calls me to help her with her problem.

Why does no one come if I have a problem?

She tells me to work and eat!

Who should talk about work ?!

She called me a 'girl'. Tell me, 'I'm a girl' ?

— You're the one who made this such a big problem.

— Me?! Nop.. you

— What did I do ?!

— You stood in the middle and did prostitute work.

You have betrayed friendship.

— Let it be so.

— Don't come to see me anymore ..!

Just run away.

 I trusted you a lot.

(I got in my hotel friend's Bike)

— He will be like a child. He doesn't even know who to talk to.

If you hate everyone like this, you will end up standing alone.

- Right now I'm just like that.

- This situation will pass ..

You have no money today. 5 more years from now, you will have bought the car.

I will look at you and ask sadly, 'Didn't even say you bought the car'.

Not everyone is always the same.

My only favorite word in the Bible

'Everything is an illusion'

I do not read the Bible much.That's the worst word for me.

'Everything is an illusion'

This too is an illusion. Here is this building, for the next 5 years only the ground will be here. Nothing is permanent..!

Do not confuse this matter with so much ..!

— I'm not confused.. Take me into that problem and let me enter..

I think I'm leaving.

I think of running away somewhere, to a place invisible to the eye.

— Your shadow will come to you.

These kinds of people, knowingly or unknowingly, are an integral part of your life. Stay still .. You can't go anywhere without this.

Your mind is just for you, you are stuck alone.

If you are bored, come to my house.

— Nop! Drop me on my Room.

— Don't smoke too much ..

(Friend's consolation speech, gave me Pease)

1.8 The nature of the dog

— This is my dog

It has been many years since I decided to maintain this.

This cannot be maintained outside.

— Is this what you kept hidden inside the bag?

— I don't know what other people's view of this is.

But, I value this more than my life.

It fulfills the needs of me. I think it gives me peace of mind

Just because I play with it, I forget all my worries and fall asleep.

— But, this dosn't look like a dog ?!

— I know. But, its actions can be felt. This is the dog you can finally do.

— Where did you get this from ?!

— It got me by the roadside. I found this to be realistic during good rainy season.

It was crying. Just like me.

— What does it eat daily ?!

— No. It is eaten only once a month. That's when it takes hunger.

I.e., on a full moon day.

— What will it do on other days?

— For a month it will be asleep. It urinate in bed.

— What else will it eat ?!

— Meat ?! It does not eat lamb, chicken or beef.

Taste the human flesh.

— Is this a terrible animal?

— No. This is a good dog. You will understand if you get used to it.

— Does it really consume human flesh ?!

— Otherwise it will bite me.

When hungry, there is no master and no friend.

— Where do you get the meat from ..?

— I will not bring. If I get someone like you, I'm brainwashed and bring them here.

— Murderous sinner.!

— I do not commit any murder. Simply watching the fun

I am a grateful master for my dog. That's all.

— In what way is that dog helpful to you ..?

— As an average human being, can one be free to do what one thinks?

Can't you ?!

But, this dog gives me it for free.

— Will you kill a man for that ?!

— Not human. Only her feet.

— Foot?

— Yes. The feet of the bulls are the most favorite part of my dog

Enjoy inch by inch.

— Will you eat it ..?

— Slowly, gnaw.., gnaw

— What will you do with the rest of the body ?!

— I will cut it into pieces and flush it in the toilet

— How many people have you killed so far?

— Every month, my dog needs paws

..For the five days before the full moon day it will be very hungry.

Every day, one foot will be needed.

It's less to eat, but more to taste.

That's why look at the tongue sticking out

(I wish he had been a close friend of mine. I have told him the secret about my dog)

— Can i paint the taste i feel ? This is subtle art

(What a bad dream. At midnight that dream disturbed my sleep.)

CHAPTER - I I

2.1 The City Life

— These are all Damaged cameras ! This cannot be fixed. Stay in your room. Just Use Anything.

— Of course!

— where is that Alcohol bottle ?!

Do you have a cigarette ?!

(We had finished the first round)

— Metropolitan life is just amazing.

Do you know how we will be there?

— Good salary ?!

— Yap! Good life ..Do you know how many women ?!

— 5 (or) 6 ..?

— All that does not count.

Started when studying 10th. Lots of aunts ..

— Auntie ?!

— Just talk. Then back to good manners, when the opportunity arises, you do not need to call.

— So, will you come only for that ?!

— Yes

— Aren't they all ashamed ?! Will there be a family for them ?!

— If we become their confidant, then family is the question mark.

— How to become trustworthy ?!

— Buy and give them their favorite. Emphasis should be placed on the main food items

They need to discuss what they are talking about willingly. Do not simply cut.

— How do we find out about their importance?

— They will ignore when talking about certain things

It is possible to keep some symptoms and learn about their intimacy.

Calling home means that we have become a very close relationship.

— Won't you get caught up in this?

— They are in danger if they find out.

They are the ones who need to be safe. We are not.

— If the relationship goes wrong, what to do ?! How to deal with it?

— Important rule 'Long-term relationship should not be included.'

— If forced?

— Have to deal with

— Will they not expect any help from you beyond sex ?!

— Do not hesitate to sin sometimes. When duty comes, they do not think about sins.

I was a second year student in college. She is my Classmate, we have no attraction. Just Friends.

One day we were discussing the study.

No one was home at the time.

She brought tea and gave it to me. The scent of the jasmine flowers she was wearing attracted me.

I touched her. She did not deny it. She closed her eyes.

Everything is over within us.

— Did your relationship not last after that?

— Lasted a few days. Then she married someone else. Not in a relationship with her now.

(I preferred to listen to intimate stories, rather than the psychological questions that arose in them.)

2.2 The Dog's First food

— Is there anyone here ?! I had come inside.

(The door locked automatically. All the lights shone like dim yellow oil lamps.)

— I know, you will surprised me.

My whole body is thrilled to see these lights.

What a smell !? It's like taking me to heaven.

— Come in slowly.

I cleaned the floor with grape seed oil

Walk slowly like a swan

Should I touch the fingers of your right hand ?!

I will take you without falling down.

— Do you have beautiful paintings on the walls ?! Are you a painter ?!

— My hobby is painting on boards.

In the face of living paintings like yours, these are just trivialities.

— This room is beautiful.

— This room has a glass bathtub.

I put apple, orange, mango, jackfruit, banana, strawberry, raspberry fruits in it and mixed it with sandalwood oil and water.

The feet leaving your shoes should be softly embedded in the glass tub.

— But, are my clothes bothersome ?!

— You do not need to take off your clothes. It spoils the nature of the painting.

Lift your feet and place them on the edge of the tub.

May the blessing of washing my feet come to me.

— Ha ... Ha .. Ha ..

— Your husband is a saint.

It is as if he has been penitent for seven generations in order to reach your benevolent feet.

— Doesn't he understand my awesomeness ? He is Useless.

— Lift the top slightly so that the knees are visible.

With the brush on the legs will be the color scheme texture.

— Are you going to paint ?!

— Brush my fingers. 'Painting' is painting with my toes from toe to toe.

Sometimes even my tongue turns into a brush.

— You are not a painter, you are a thief.

— I have never seen such feet like sculpture before. Introduce your secret to your husband.

— Do not talk about him

— it is the nature of the servant to realize the condition of the thirsty and seek and help.

I felt your thirst in your walk.

— Is that why you often come to the store to buy cigarettes ?!

Ha .. Ha ..

I have lost my beauty. I have two daughters. I'm getting old.

My eye sight blurred.

— I am going to blindfold you and take you to the gates of heaven.

— Take it as soon as possible.

— This is the heaven of the mind

The time for painting the feet with the tongue was approaching.

— Ha .. hum .. be shy .. slow

Hey don't bite. It hurts.

Please... hey.. what is this ..?

— There is nothing to be afraid of.

 This is my dog.

It's got your feet so caught up in it.

— What the hell is this ..?

— Just give your feet to my dog's appetite.

— What the fu**

— Be extremely hungry for it. The full moon day is close.

Please cooperate.

 (I hit her on the skull and made her faint.)

2.3 Suicide is self-liberation

— Everyone screamed at what you said.

I didn't even take it seriously.

Mainly your sister, your best friends everyone..!

— Why did he come here?

— Has come to stop a friend trying to commit suicide

— I'm going to do it

— Until yesterday, you were trying to escape to an unseen place, are you trying to commit suicide?

— Why did he come here ..?

— No wonder someone who cares about you comes and meets you

— Will you post a suicide attempt on Instagram, facebook ?!

— There is a reason.

Someone who looks at me again will think and insult my suicide note

I decided to escape the ridicule and die.

— Why do you have to die?

— No use

— You do not see the world as far as I can see.

 'Take it money'

— I will return this.

— I don't know how you are..

..But, if I were in your position, I would not hesitate to ask you for help.

— This is not the first time for me.

I have already tried it twice.

— I know

This is the last decision that cowards make.

Maybe you are dead, I will come to your grave and write like this

 'He is not my friend. He is a woman. No wonder he committed suicide '

 (I smiled unknowingly)

— It's true,

..I will cry for you if you die naturally.

And I will come to your grave every day and sing floral greetings.

Remember my grave sayings whenever suicidal thoughts appear.

'I tell you the truth, I will come to your grave from nowhere and write thus'.

2.4 The image of beauty

— How are you having fun?

— I draw

— Have you been awake all night and drawing so much?

— That curiosity has stuck with me ever since I saw those Zibu Symbol pictures.

I chose the feet

..How does that feel when you touch the earth as a child and its feet! ?!

What do you call that moment when she tries to absorb the earth and stand on her own two feet?

 Is it arrogant? Beautiful? Or the beauty of nature?

— I've been thinking about you ever since you fought me

— I'm sorry dude

— Forgive me too

If an artist leaves this world it is a disaster for this world.

— Invaluable artist is a gift to the trash

— Do you see that girl next door every day?

— Her feet are not gravitational.

— Pardon ?!

— It fades with explosion.

It's more common in older women.

Adolescents do not properly care for the feet.

— You know something ?!

— What ?!

— Missing a woman in this area.

— Oh ...!

— They may be running a shop in this area.

— I don't know ..

— Look at that girl. You have to use the ladder to touch her head.

— He is her boyfriend

— But, good shape.

Her house should be nearby!

 (I looked behind them as they passed us. There were no cracks in her feet. I kept looking at the path she had taken until her feet disappeared.)

— How could she have grown so tall. ?

— Food ?! How old is she?

— 25 ..?

— Nope. There will be only 18

— I can't believe it ..

— Rich people world is different.

2.5 Me and My dog

— I was able to satisfy your hunger today.

I hope you will fulfill my need according to the agreement we made before you went to sleep.

(The dog jumped for joy)

— I can feel the blood rushing across the room. I am going to spray perfume and clean.

I will soak the sandalwood and spray it all over the room..The scent of sandalwood fills the room whenever the room is cold.

In the bathroom, I have increased the level of acid.

I had to take great pains for your one day meal.

'You go in the bag' !

I would have been glad if you were a cannibal.

But you are a foot-eating animal.

Where do I cover the rest of the body?

(There was a knock on the door.)

— Hide, I'll see who it is.

Tell me what you want?

— Is alcohol available?

— No Available now.

— Please try

— Actually it is not available at the moment.

— Call us if you get, okay ?!

(I closed the door and came inside)

— Hey .. are you inside?

(Dog jumps)

— I saw a girl yesterday

She was like an angel. Her foot was 9 inches long

(The dog jumped back.)

— But she had a boyfriend.

(Dog tired)

— Don't you worry!

I will finish that

Their pairing was so awesome.

She went on muttering something.

Feeling we have 'Run out of gas' emotionally.

Her gait was like going and touching the sky.

Her hair, which hung like a ponytail, blossomed in her gait.

She is about 11 feet past me.. ..I felt the shock of the earth in me.

(Someone knocked on the door)

— Who are You ?

— Sir, I have come to Resume for Hotel work

— You do not have a job yet.

..You can't stay here.

I am HR

— You know my friend very well. I rely on his recommendation

— Chef Is this room enough for you?

Tell me if you don't like it, there is still a lot of accommodations

(This accommodation seemed unwelcome to him.)

— Tell your friend to contact me.

The trash can is overflowing. No one to clean this up ?!

Cigarette liquor is not allowed here.

Work on the hotel will begin only when Lockdown is End.

No problem about you staying and Write a letter.

2.6 Need is the stimulus of desire

— Did you hear the camera in a hurry ?!

— I think I can do Photoshoot again.

I am going to combine painting and photography together.

— Good. Can i come too

— Don't bother me for a few days!

It is enough to come only when I call.

— Did you find the watch with me ?!

..It's in your room. I think I forgot

— I'll find it and call you

— I urgently need it

— Can't. I will give it to you as soon as possible.

It's time for me. I need to start my work.

— Are you sure you want a camera?

— Yes.

— That camera belongs to your sister. If you sell it, you will not get much money.

If you want money, ask me ... I will give

— I don't want to beg anyone

— What a rush for money.

Everything is expensive

Selling is not a good sign of survival.

...Unless you already have a grudge against her, this job is unnecessary.

— If I had a job this time, I wouldn't be doing this

I know you will tell her this thing… Say, 'I'll refund the camera'

— Your dad kicked you out of the house. Do you know why?

It is because of engaging in such irresponsible acts.

— What is liability?

 I am his son. He did not understand me.

You are my friend. Stop your argument only with advice.

Do not interfere in my personal life.

Don't come to see me anymore

2.7 I saw her

— Hi. I saw you in this area yesterday, with your boyfriend

— Who ?!

(She adjusts her nose glasses)

— Hmm.. last night, at the ice cream shop

— He's not my boyfriend. Just Classmate Only.

— Oh.. Sorry.. Can you collaborate with me on a new project?

We need young couples like you.

— Sorry I don't like it.

— Its ok. Find out about that project. It depends on social awareness

There are opportunities to be popular.

— No...But ..

— You can think generously and say your answer.

Can you come with me to the office?

— I have no problem. But, will he agree with this point? I do not know

(My eyes were on her feet.)

— Who told you I was interested in this?

— It's you.

..I saw your Instagram page yesterday.

That photo with the dress you wore yesterday was so cute

— Ha ha ..

— Your style of dress and appearance will reflect your intuition.

— Doesn't that tell you what the project is ?!

— It is Conceptual Art Photography. That project transmits human instincts through photography.

I am going to attach the sketch and the photo.

— Can I do this properly? Does not seem to.

..Because I'm just a begainer

— This project is completely confidential. It's free to your liking.

 Mistakes have full permission to happen.

2.8 It will be beastly

— Did you hear the bag?

— Oh..Thanks Dude. come in.

I have been Searching for a watch for long time.

No one is likely to have stolen it.

I would have forgotten somewhere...

..I will definitely search and find.

— Can I help you too?

— Sure

— No one in this lockdown is wandering around like crazy without a job.

— That's true.

— Some people sell and eat things at home.

Some have even started stealing.

— Now what did you say ?! Are you talking about me?

— No. I'm not talking about you.

I told him about common social behavior.

We should have gotten a government job.

Monthly salary would not have been an issue.

— That's true.

Even in this predicament, they do not know where the money is coming from ..?!

— Must be rich, otherwise must be a government official !

— I do not think it is wrong to steal or loot at this time.

For most people, life is a struggle

— Saw a news in the morning.

It's news about a man who killed his friend for money

— Really ?!

— He put the body in pieces in the toilet and flush it. Two weeks later he was arrested on suspicion and interrogated.

'Cut into 230 pieces'

He has done it very cleverly. Only after he himself admitted the truth did the police get relief.

Still unable to fully capture the corpse.

— People have become beasts.

— What is that ?!

— That...

— Oh its Textile shop toy.

Why are you holding this?

— Nothing like you expected.. I keep this for my artistic inspiration.

CHAPTER - III

3.1 The Fragrance Garden

— Do I need a kilo of jasmine flowers ?!

Untouched flowers should be combed..

..I would be very happy to get it as dried flowers

Lily flowers with stem leaves are essential.

— You can only buy such a variety if you go to the garden.

It's just a florist here.

— Where is the flower garden ?!

— Why do you need those flowers ?!

— The most popular flower among the flowers is the lily of the valley.

I can distinguish the individual taste in each from its magazine to the end.

From evening to morning the scent of the flower would permeate her mane as it adorned her bed.

If the lily flowers reveal the true scent of femininity

The scent created by combining vanilla, cinnamon and marigold together will reveal the true scent of men.

I want to reach that fragrant garden.

— Are you a researcher?

— No. I need 15 types of perfumes.

It contains 10 types of seeds and 5 types of fruits.

Flowers like Jasmine, Lily, Rose, Lily, Lilac, Lavender..

..Fragrances like vanilla, cinnamon, saffron, ginger, musk turmeric, sandalwood, dried tobacco, potina, chilli are also required.

— Lily flower What is it? Can't get it there ?!

— Also they called 'Lily of the valley'.

The Bible says that it reflects the heart of the Lord.

I will mention lilies as the queen in fragrance. I am not a researcher. I am a painter.

— Do you give importance to perfumes ?!

— They may be chemically mixed molecules. I like to get the classic real scent.

— Can you create perfume ?!

— Did you know that the material obtained from the pot full of musk yellow, sandalwood and lily of the valley?

'Want to identify yourself alone on a crowded Paris city street?'

This fragrance will declare you the protector of heaven.

— Why 10 types of seeds ?!

— Pomegranate, grape, nostril, avocado seed, fig seed, soy beans, pumpkin seed, walnut nuts, watermelon seeds and cashew seeds.

All seeds are aphrodisiacs

Let them cool under the fig tree overnight.

Serve with watermelon and grape juices,

Eat ripe fruits,

I stand as a passerby waiting for the world to refresh and watch the fun.

(I found my way to the Fragrance garden)

3.2 The Conceptional Art

— So glad you changed your mind. I had no idea you would be here so soon.

Let me give you the table of terms..

..Sign this contract crystal.

— How did you find this room ?!

I hope you are not caught in the eyes of the defender.

— We came here without even knowing the family.

— Won't you get caught on the way back?

— Let's deal with lying.

Let's say we went outside and discussed education.

— Good! Let's get started ?!

I am going to guide you every moment.

 'Conceptual photography' is fine art. There are a lot of differences between this and other types of photography. There are differences.

 A hand-picked photographer in this field, he loves to play with his course..

 ..I mean, let's keep this as a playground. Suppose a kind of game is played in it. You and I are the athletes who are going to take part in this.

 Respecting the rules I am going to record the game you play on my camera.

You do not need to suffer. Join hands with your hands.

First you have to have a mutual bond between you.

— is.. a little shy…

— Come on..

— Nope!

— Conceptual Photography is

There is no such thing as 'burying your face in the meadow and defining humanity'.

This is a fine art. These are not easy to understand.

Related to natural fine arts. It keeps us and other beings connected to each other.

It is, 'not as obvious as a human body buried face in the meadow'

The trick is to connect the blood vessels that run through the human body with the rivers that flow through the earth.

First you two, relax yourself in a room..

..You can sleep. Take a bath. Let's eat. You can do your favorite thing.

I'm not going to force you.

(As soon as the two of them entered the separate room, I began to notice the clock hands. After a while, they slapped and left)

— We have no interest in this. We are leaving.

— But, you have signed the contract. Forgot it ?!

— That's true. But, Not today. It may be possible another day.

(I noticed a lot of changes in the way they behaved.)

3.3 The Difficult Situation

— She's just standing outside.

— Who ?!

— If you do not take it wrong, are you waiting for me at the bar?

— Why ?!

— Get a nice view there. You rest there for half an hour.

— I'm waiting right here.

— That girl has come with me.

— Do you have a girlfriend ?!

— You can still say that. You know her very well.

She smiles as we pass each day.

— I do not remember exactly.!

— This is the time when my girlfriend is not in town.

You go upstairs and relax. In just half an hour, everything is over.

Go upstairs without question.

  (The room was locked as soon as I left)

— Hello, hmm .. what are you doing ?!

Do not touch anything inside ..!

— That textile toy ?! Will do nothing

I'm going to turn off the phone.

  [It is asleep. If you wake up, both of you will be killed, God save you.]

At three-quarters of an hour, they left.

— Hey, what are you doing on the doorstep? Didn't go upstairs

I told him to rest himself on the floor.

I'm going to drop her off at home.

— Wait, where is it? My guess is wrong. God!

— What are you asking about?

Will you be under the bed? Kitchen or balcony ?!

  Oh God !!

Hungry for it. It is as if the hunger has gone unchecked.

— What are you drying?

— It violates the agreement we made.

It definitely needs my help.

 Would it have jumped out the window ?!

  No chance. It just keeps moving and moving. Can't climb the wall..

..Maybe, the door would have opened and gone out ?!

I was just outside

— Are you clear about what you are talking about?

— It's a busty dog.

Did you see that?

I found out. It would have penetrated into the bathroom..

..Where would it have gone through the toilet ?!

The septic tank would have gone and joined.

— Why not crawl to the other toilet?

— Correct. Are you helping me ?!

3.4 The missing dog

— Excuse Me Sir .. We have come in search of a missing dog.

— Dogs in the apartment, do not raise. Do not you know

— Sorry Sir !

Screaming alone on the side of the road.

— Little dog ?!

— Yes Sir ..

— I do not see anything like that

  (We knocked on the door of the next room)

— We were looking for a dog.

— kya ? (What) Kutha (He is North Indian)

— yep. Small kutha (dog)

— nahi (Nope

(We knocked on the door of the next house)

— A dog has gone missing with us.

— Which colour ?

— Its Black. Black color.

— My daughter has a dog toy. She said she brought it down

— It's a living dog.

— I do not see anything like that

(Heard the sound of a puppy from somewhere.)

— Did you hear that? That's the sound of the puppy.

I think it will be upstairs.

(Next House..)

— Did you see that dog?

— Which dog? I'm a dog myself.

The embarrassment I get stuck with my wife is more disgusting than a dog.

— I'm sorry ! We have moved house. It sounds like a husband-wife problem.

(Next House..)

— What do you want ..?!

— Sir .. A similar puppy is missing from ours.

— Really? I just picked up this dog yesterday.

  Screaming alone on the side of the road.

Is that yours ?!

— This is not my dog.

— You called yourself a black dog ?!

— It's black, but it turns green when eaten.

— Will it turn green ?!

— Yes. It's a green dog.

— Do you have a green dog?

Is it a foreign dog?

— It's like a dog, but it's not a dog

— Did you raise a dog? Did you raise any other animal?

— That's the dog.

 I found it in the opposite room.

It might even be that bar guy's dog.

— Is he his own?

— I don't know but, chances are. It made me a deal.

— Agreement? How can a dog talk ?!

3.5 It Was a Dream

— Nice to meet you again. Didn't your friend come here ?!

— We do not always agree. We have a lot of things to talk about and resolve.

— Of course.

— I'm not feeling well. Some guilt burns in me!

Can I collaborate on your project alone?

— ofcourse...sure

 But, this is an embarrassing situation for me. I can't do this alone with you. - Is it all over ?!

As far as you are concerned, nothing has happened..

..In the midst of a chaotic and perishing world,

I am an ordinary artist looking for beautiful soft feet.

This world is doomed by the superiority of the arts.

The arts have crossed their boundaries.

They, too, have lost their uniqueness.

I have hope.

'A beautiful footprint will lead to the restoration of a ruined art form'.

— Isn't that luck on my feet?

— Yes.. Will you give me the opportunity to wash your feet? It violated my contracts. I feel like a brushless painter.

— I can't do this alone.

— Try.

— I can't.. Leave. Let me go outside until I get bile.

3.6 The lost dog

— For a long time a dream reappeared and haunted me.

— It can be for good or for bad.

— I believe there are possibilities for something bad to happen.

That's what came from my dream. I have expressed it as an image of a dream.

— It…That dog.?

Are you saying it came from a dream ?!

— No. I consider it a dream that I got that dog.

When I first saw it, I had no tension or fear.

— Have you seen it many times in your dreams ?!

— Yes, it's a talkative dog that behaves smarter than humans.

— Does it speak ..?

— It communicates with our mind.

 ..It's a dog that wanders with nostalgia, as if it's always stuck out its tongue in saliva.

It is natural for anyone who sees it to be infected with the desire to achieve it.

— How to search in public about a strange dog ?!

They will not believe, except to call us crazy.

— We can try to diagnose ourselves with its symptoms.

— Where to look ?! What to look for ?!

— We don't need to say anything.

Let's search every room.We will search inside each house as per his wish.

— No tragedy, as you say, has ever happened,

Then why should we take pains to search ..?!

Not only that, it is better to leave it as it is.

Because, if this is true, don't forget that you are also an accomplice ..!

Will have to face the consequences.

— But, it will increase the number of casualties.

If you try to walk in it wisely, you may end up losing yourself.

— Don't act like a good man..!

— The weakness of each person's selfishness is the strength of that dog.

It is a well-understood animal that understands the weaknesses of others. We need to know ourselves before it catches the eye of others.

— Lastly, you will not only share the contract with me ?!

 (I smiled and walked away)

3.7 An Investigation

— So you can not work in that hotel, is that so ?!

— I have given Resume, Sir

— What is your hometown?

— This is my hometown, sir.

— Then you have to go home..?! Why are you here ..?!

— Family problem Sir.

Dad and me disagree.

— How many days have you stayed here?

— One month

— Are you a Photographer ?!

— No Sir, I am a painter.

— How many years has your friend been working there?

— Approximately 4 years sir

— Are you the only one staying in the room?

— Yes Sir.

— Will anyone else come to the room ?! Any of the girls?

— No Sir.

— Do you have a habit of drinking alcohol ..?

— No. Sir.

— Then why are there so many bottles here ?!

— May have been used by those who have stayed here before me Sir.

— Write your mobile number and home address in this paper.

— Generous Sir !

— Don't get me wrong.

Three women are still missing in the area.

 This is only for a week.

That is why we are investigating persons who remain Unwanted.

I hope you will cooperate.

— Of course Sir.

3.8 The foot of God

— How did the curse of the foot touch you?

— It wasn't a curse in the beginning.

I could not see his eyes with my bare eyes.

There was guilt in me. I stood with my head bowed.

He felt that anyone who could not see was not worthy.

What can I do! ?!

I considered it a blessing to see his feet.

— Is he unable to understand your mind ?!

— He is the only one who understands my mind. I had the opportunity to worship the feet of God.

I took the scent of every flower of the planet and prayed every night.

One night I went to the garden to pick flowers.

There are no new flowers to worship from me. Flowers already worshiped cannot be submitted again at the feet of God.

I decided to pursue the next garden..

..We could not find innovative flowers anywhere..

..I fell asleep in the garden that night.

— Did you show indifference ..?!

— Yes, I got the curse because of the negligence I showed

I wandered around looking for fragrant flowers, not paying attention to the fragrant fragrances.

I decided that I could no longer do puja with perfumes.

But, I could not see the feet of God.

He is gone. Dissatisfied with me he went elsewhere.

I wandered all over the world in search. In his image, the foot of God is invisible, except the feet of men.

Those feet are clear.

No explosions. Clean.

The difference between the inner foot and the upper foot is indistinguishable.

Furs free at fingertips.

There was a thin radius at the edge of the heel.

— Those feet are definitely women's feet.!

— Yes. In their innate arrogance. I feel the pure soul of God.

My vision was towards the earth.

My purpose is to identify the feet.

My goal is to find God's feet.

My search is to reach God's feet

CHAPTER - IV

4.1 The Bathroom Cleaner

— I have come to clean your bathroom.

— Go straight and return to Wright

Where are you from ?!

Don't you know how to clean the bathroom ?!

— You know after I cleaned up.

— Have you studied anything?

What would the country be like if all the educated people came to wash the bathroom ?!

— its Fate. Only time will tell

— Wait a minute. Did you eat anything?

 (I thoroughly inspected the room before cleaning the toilet. There were no signs of the dog being there.

The dog's skin is smooth and fluid. Of course I can identify the path it has traversed. I guess he will live here alone)

— Whatever it is, you should not ask 100 rupees to wash the bathroom!

During this time, even a vegetable seller sells the fruit at a profit of ten rupees.

Don't miss your top. it is all fate.

 (It looks like he was a civil servant.

Probably a federal employee. I can feel it in his contract speech.)

— No matter what the problem, do not cheat only on the stomach! Hold it.

4.2 The Dangerous City

— You missed me!

'I am not selfish'

— I'm not a good man, I'm not a decent one. I guess I obviously live it.

— You are not alone.

I can better understand the suffering that comes with being abandoned.

— Don't you think what I'm saying is nonsense ?!

— He was caught by the police.

— Who ?!

— Kidnapper of missing women.

He has been living in the apartment next door for two years., I doubted you.

— But, Why ?!

— I thought you gave your dog a feast. The culprit has pleaded guilty.

Only one thing he said agrees with what you said

— What ?!

— He would have said that there was a motive behind committing those crimes. He, like you, has said that he has contracted with an animal.

He said that he had been provoked by a devil and that he was hungry and that it had incited him to commit those crimes.

— That's that dog.

— He even killed a woman last week.

He needs a woman's body every month.

He has been making similar sacrifices for almost a year and a half.

— God !!

— The funny thing is, on the same day that your dog went missing, his dog also went missing.

— Had there been two dogs ?!

— The city itself is talking today about a racist force.

His claim that he was not solely responsible for his crime has sent shockwaves through the city.

Sounds like nonsense doesn't it ?! I trust you completely.

My guess is that the mentality of those who are lonely may have invited such a satanic companion.

I guess, Not one but two lots of dogs roam this city.

4.3 The Breeding animal

— Okay.. I'm leaving. It is clear that I am not the only one responsible for the crimes that took place.

So I have no job here. Only now do I feel relaxed

— Have you not been complicit in the crime?

— Many like me are involved in this.

There have been two dogs we know of. In this city alone, imagine how many more dogs there will be.

The outside world does not even know the crime I committed.

Understand..it's not like the dog on earth.

It's different.

It can confuse humans. What if everyone like me was contracted ?!

No one will come forward to betray it.

— Maybe, if it does not behave as per the contract? As it happened to you..

— Humans do not like the other. Humans are expected to show loyalty to one animal. It only eats food 5 days a month.

'It tastes like feet'

It...It will expel eggs.

— What ?!

— Yes, it lays eggs..

..As it sneezes it will expel the eggs.

The cumulus fluid comes out in clumps. It is full of mucus-like fluid.

As the temperature of the air increases, the eggs hatch and hatch.

— Where are those puppies ?!

— They are moving towards a new place where they can live.

— It uses humans as a tool to give shelter on this earth to a strange creature.

 (Suddenly a noise)

— What are you two talking about? That's my bag. Why did you take it ..?

— He was the one who used to stay in this room. The guy works at the Hotel Bar.

4.4 The weakness of man

— Where did you get that dog?

— Just like how you got there, from that room..

I came here just like you. I maintained it for about six months.

'It is a bland animal'

— Whom will you sacrifice for its hunger?

— I will not give any food to it. I cheated on it.

— Cheated, How ?!

— It commanded that it needed a human body.

The body of a young adult woman was deliberately mutilated. I can't wander for a young adult woman.

Nude pictures I brought some prints and pasted them on the wall all over the room.

— Do you have this textile toy too ?!

— Why did you take the stitch ?!

Aren't you ashamed to touch intimate things ..?

— Did you cheat on that dog with this toy ?!

— That dog is so smart.

One day it realized the thing I was cheating on. I do not understand what to do.

I poured wine on it. Keep it quiet. But, Daily I could not keep it under the influence of alcohol.

One day I decided I could kill it. It kept motivating me to commit crimes.

—Then why did you leave without killing ?!

— I had agreed to pay a lot of money. Maybe if it dies I would have stopped getting paid.

I dreamed of becoming a millionaire.

A family problem in hometown. I went to town and had to settle. I can't take it with me.

I was put under anesthesia and put to sleep and left for the city.

I guess I could have arrived sooner, but at the height of the trouble I had to go to the police station.

— None of those agreements are valid anymore. It has multiplied. It is no longer going down the street and hunting humans.

— Will all the animals be hungry at the same time?

— Nope. Have you escaped from prison?

— Such a death is bizarre. Check out this newspaper article.

4.5 The Society of People

— Look here it's fun.

— Can you tell me how reliable the message you have received on your mobile is ?!

— Oh.. Sure..

This was taken from the evening news page

— So are people going to unite anymore ?!

 Together..crowded in one place ?!

— Yes.. that is the only solution to this problem.

— Do you think people are crazy?

Those who said stay alone and stay awake now say stay together.

— This is a reaction to isolating people.
This is now becoming a nationwide problem.

— People have helped the beast.

..Fearing the rat, they got trapped by the tiger.

Do you believe the virus was spread by someone who ate rat meat in a corner somewhere in China ?! We are close to the truth.

Let's keep the spread real ..

How did it come to be?

Could it be a virus that was deliberately spread in the lab by bad scientists ?!

Or will it be the work of that beast ?!

— Maybe.

Fearing a small racist virus, people began to flee.

During the day, people were afraid to see each other and reached inside the house individually.

The problem of being inside is greater than the problem of being outside.

— I was looking for a relaxed life.

That's what I wanted..

..I was relieved to hear from that beast. That's the deal I made. I have been sleeping peacefully for several days.

— What do you consider peace.

It has been almost 2 years since it was identified as an animal.

It's time to wake up.

4.6 Strength And Weakness

— Did you hear that noise ?!

— Oh my Gosh!

— Pick up any weapon available immediately.

Close the ear completely.

— How are we going to destroy it ..?!

— We will use the cell phone to keep up with each other. Even vision can distract us. Our focus needs to be entirely on the goal.

— There's a girl screaming.

  (We ran in the direction of the scream)

— Don't be afraid..which direction did it go ?!

— That toilet has leaked inside. It sucked the blood out of me.

— We rush to the hospital

 It's time for us.

You go inside the next room, look at the toilet to be there ..You go down and see.

(We scattered and ran)

— Why do all these people look like crazy ?!

— It has to be somewhere just here. It controls the Mind.

Everyone disconnect cell phones. We will no longer communicate in sign language.

They are all standing in the same direction. All of these are connected together.

— what are you saying ?!

— They are waiting for its command.

Television is running in everyone's homes.

— Is every person controlled via TV channel?

— No, No.. Everyone is connected by the message..

..All these idols will start functioning as soon as the instruction is laid.

— Let's divert its attention.

— Is it possible?

— It diverts our attention. If that is possible, then so be it.

— It needs a human body and that too a woman's body. How is this possible?

— It has multiplied, and now it can live here freely.

It no longer needs breeding. Only human bodies are sufficient to satisfy hunger..Otherwise apparently not hunting like this.

— But, why?

— It thinks to shape this world just like itself.

Guess to design as per his liking.

(We decided to get out of that dark room)

4.7 The Naked Bodies

— Look at this .. You know what I said is funny.

There is no other way out of this.

— Let's inflate the blood along the way. To place it with us,

I Mean, let us come to the room.

— That's right, it's back to the room, how are we going to deal with it ?!

Shall we close our eyes?

Should I pack my ears?

What else are we going to shut down ..?!

I have been a month.

I am well aware of the paragraph on Next activities.

Can't fight against anyone who confronts it, except the stagnant Nippons.

That's the people, like them.

— We have the weapon, and as soon as it enters the room, we will attack it.

— It will fool us.

Think about it, how do you do all this cool stuff?

Showing a nude photo.

It needs our admiration for now.

It is looking for an independent way to achieve its own principles.

— Can do nude photo?

— May turn naked.

— Naked?

— Yes, it has an extreme attraction to our body.

Just as we enjoy an idol, so we enjoy our body.

Beyond the naked body, there is no other way to distract it.

— Does it think to break civilization with us ?!

— It's selfish.

— We are selfish.

It made us weak, to its advantage. That's all.

Describes the naked body as a poet.

— But, is it to leave anyone alive !?

— I made a mistake. its Our mistake.

t wanted a place that was not civilized.

It is very rare to see parts of the uncivilized body behind the civilization, looking at the whole body inside its blanket.

— Our only thought in civilization is sexual thoughts.

— So, that's what it wanted.

This is because a dog does not try to restrain his body inside his shirt.

— we can conquer nudity.

(We stood naked. We felt it enter the cock room)

— It spit in the mouth. It will not hit us.

— What the hell.. it makes me laugh.

— Stand still without moving.

— Does it hear what we're talking about?

— No. Let it be sex Mood

_ Do you have a desire to reproduce ?!

— Fear not, it will do us no good.

— This is like Oral Sex.

— It lays eggs behind itself, enjoying us.

— Is it going to reach the core ?!

— This is the perfect opportunity. Take that needle and pierce the middle head.

 It will take some time to curl up.

Until then stand like a statue of silence.

— I'm embarrassed. If a girl had reddened this, I would have been so happy.

— This is also a female dog.

— Don't talk crazy, this is a beast ..

(When it got drunk, we executed our plan)

— Now what happened to this beast.

— What do you usually do? The human corpse?

— I will flush the toilet.

— Cut into pieces and flush.

— This is not your dog,

Why not regret it later.?!

— If it was a dog with me, it would come hammering at my leg.

It takes feet.

— Like destroying this, destroying everything?

What is the government's decision for this ..?!

— I Think using atomic bomb

— We are the ones who will be affected by it..

— They don't care about that.

4.8 Extermination of the beast

(The world is being saved from animals. People have started their struggle together as a community..

..However, people continue to have trouble communicating with each other because of the fear that he may be a slave to the beast)

— I'm so glad I got the job. I promise I will do this work politely.

I feel that the dissatisfaction I had with relationships is fading a little.

— so happy.? Do you have an ID card?

— No. I have to pick it up from now on.

— Pick up as soon as possible. It is a sign of your human rights. If the tent of animals continues on earth, the only reliable solution for fellow human beings is the identity card.

— I know. I care about your feet.

(People are recovering from deadly disease and are trapped by deadly beasts. We were able to kill some creatures, but they occupy most of the hosts where humans live)

— I guess I've lived so far without grammar.

I dreamed that normal life would return after Lockdown.

But, this is a harder situation than that.

I currently have a job in the recovery workplace. I plan to provide a good service

But, that beast within me can wake up at any time.

Its hunger lasts only 5 days in a month. I plan to spend those 5 days alone.

I have felt many times that the beast has infiltrated me. If it comes out of me, I will die

I do not know how many more days I will spend hiding my inner self from the government and the community.

Until then I can move freely in public.

- You must have heard about my friends. They have returned to their normal lives. But they always want to escape from that hidden situation. One day, we will work together again. I am obliged to remember my family at this time.

THE END